The Boxcar Children Mysteries

THE CANDY
FACTORY MYSTERY

created by
GERTRUDE CHANDLER WARNER

Illustrated by Hodges Soileau

SCHOLASTIC INC.
New York Toronto London Auckland Sydney
New Delhi Mexico City Hong Kong Buenos Aires

Activities by Rebecca Gomez
Activity Illustrations by Alfred Giuliani

ISBN 0-439-35374-2

12 11 10 9 8 7 6 5 4 3   2 3 4 5 6 7/0

Printed in the U.S.A.   40
First Scholastic printing, April 2002

Contents

CHAPTER 1

Watch Out!

On a cold winter night, in a big white house, the four Alden children and their cousin, Soo Lee, sat in front of a crackling fire. Grandfather was in his favorite chair. He was finishing up the last piece of coconut cake the family housekeeper, Mrs. McGregor, had made. Watch, the family dog, lay at Grandfather's feet, waiting for a few crumbs to fall his way.

"Now it's your turn to act out a charade," Jessie Alden told Benny.

"What's a charade?" five-year-old Soo

Lee asked. She was still a little new at the games her older cousins played.

"It's a guessing game," Benny answered. He was a year older than Soo Lee and loved all kinds of games, especially charades. "For candy charades, we pick a message printed on one of our candy hearts. Then we try and make everybody guess what it says. Only we can't use words, not even one, just funny faces and motions."

"Oh, I get it," Soo Lee said. "Henry's candy heart said, *Hug Me*. That's why he hugged me, right?"

"Right," twelve-year-old Jessie said. "And Violet's candy heart said, *Be Mine*. That's why she pretended to sting us like a bee and pointed to herself. *Be Mine*. Now it's Benny's turn."

"If he has any candy hearts left," fourteen-year-old Henry said.

The Alden children loved a noisy game of charades. When Grandfather's friend Mrs. Winkles sent up boxes of candy message hearts from her factory in Pennsylvania, it was the first thing they'd thought of.

Benny dumped his candy hearts into a bowl. "Good thing Mrs. Winkles sent us lots more candy hearts. This box is practically empty."

Mrs. McGregor looked up from the sweater she was knitting. "How can you have room for candy hearts after eating such a big piece of my coconut cake?"

Benny patted his stomach. "Don't worry, Mrs. McGregor. I always leave room for candy," Benny said. "Okay, I'm ready."

He picked up a heart and read the message to himself. A puzzled look passed over his face. He scrunched his eyebrows for a long time. Finally, he walked over to the doorway, where Watch's leash was hanging.

Watch raced over to Benny.

"*Doggone!*" Henry yelled. "Is that what your candy heart says?"

Poor Watch waited. Benny still had the leash in his hand.

Benny pointed to Watch, then to the door.

"*Out? Stay Out?*" Jessie guessed. "Never mind. That doesn't make sense. Candy hearts don't say things like that."

Benny held up Watch's leash again and pointed to the door.

Watch began to whine. He didn't have to guess what Benny was doing — a leash meant a walk.

"*Watch? Out?*" ten-year-old Violet cried. "Does your candy heart say, *Watch Out*?"

Benny broke into a big grin. "That's it!" he cried, handing his candy heart to Violet to pass around. "Read it. See, it says, *Watch Out*!"

Violet looked at the candy heart in surprise. Benny was right — it really did say, *Watch Out*! She passed it around to the rest of the children so they could see the odd message.

"That's a strange message to print on a candy heart," Grandfather said. "It must be a mistake. I wonder if Mrs. Winkles knows about this."

Benny poured the rest of his candy hearts onto the coffee table. He turned them over one by one. Now that he knew how to read, he liked to read everything, from street signs to cereal boxes to candy hearts.

"Look. A few other hearts in this box have strange messages, too. Some of them say, *Trouble*, *Danger Ahead*, *Go Away*, *Beware*, *Warning*."

"Remember the chocolate mice Mrs. Winkles sent?" Henry asked. "They didn't have any tails."

Grandfather scratched his chin. "Yes, that was odd as well. I couldn't bring myself to tell Rose Winkles about those. I didn't want to upset her — and I thought the shipment might have just been damaged by accident. But these candy hearts seem to be quite a different matter."

Benny had an idea. "Hey, what if they're for April Fools' Day or Halloween? Maybe the messages are supposed to be for fun."

Grandfather shook his head. "Oh, that wouldn't be something Rose would do — not at all. Her longtime customers wouldn't find these candy hearts amusing. I'm certain of that."

"All the candy she sends us at holidays are

sweet and pretty," Violet said. "Even the chocolate mice with no tails."

"You know, children," Grandfather said, "I've been meaning to see how Rose is doing. She's always inviting us to visit. I'm sure she would enjoy seeing your cheery young faces. She doesn't have much family left."

The children stared into the fire for a few moments. They knew what it was like to be cut off from relatives. After their own parents died, they had lived on their own in a boxcar in the woods without any other family but each other. Luckily, Grandfather had searched for them and brought them back to live in his big white house. Now they couldn't imagine living apart from Grandfather and all their other wonderful Alden relatives.

"When Seth Winkles died, he left the factory to his wife, Rose," Grandfather went on. "After that, his brother and sister wouldn't have anything to do with her. They were upset that Seth didn't leave the factory to them. Rose has nieces and nephews on Seth's side whom she's never met, even though they don't live very far away."

"Maybe we can be Mrs. Winkles's nieces and nephews," Violet said in her serious way.

"And then we would have a candy-making aunt!" said Benny with a grin.

"Yes, I'm sure Rose would like that very much," Grandfather said. "She's like an aunt the way she remembers to send you children candy for all the holidays. I'll give her a call right now."

"I'd like to take a look at the other candy boxes she sent," Henry suggested. "There's something very mysterious about those candy hearts in Benny's box."

The children went off to the pantry to find the rest of the candy. They poured all the hearts onto the kitchen table.

"Looks as if just a couple boxes have those strange messages," Henry said after everyone checked all the candy hearts. "At least there weren't too many bad ones."

Grandfather came back into the kitchen. "Well, we'll be visiting Mrs. Winkles next week. She especially asked if you'd like to lend a hand with making her candies. What do you say?"

Benny picked up a pink heart and read the message to everyone: "*2 Good 2 B True.*"

CHAPTER 2

A Chocolate Mystery

A week later, the Aldens were on their way to Winkles Candy Factory. Shortly after Grandfather turned off the busy highway, the children began to see smaller towns and green farms with white farm buildings, windmills, and barns full of hay.

"Wow!" Benny said. "I counted fifty-two cows so far."

"This area is full of cows, Benny," Grandfather said, smiling. "Even *you* won't be able to count them all."

"And all those cows are full of milk to make chocolate," Benny said. "I hope I won't be able to count all the chocolate candies, either, when we get to Winkles Candy Factory."

A few minutes later, Grandfather came to a stop in front of a tidy two-story brick building. Benny read aloud the pink lettering on the large hand-painted sign: "*Winkles Candy Factory — Making Holiday Candy since 1922. Visitors Welcome.*"

Grandfather rolled down his window and took a deep breath. "Just follow your noses, children."

Violet sniffed the air. "Mmm. It's like chocolate perfume."

The children headed straight to the small candy shop attached to the factory building. Through the window they saw a pink-cheeked, white-haired woman in a spotless white smock. She was cutting into a tray of fudge.

A small bell over the door rang when Benny pushed it open. "The Aldens are here!"

"And so is the candy!" the cheery woman said, offering them all some fudge. "I recognize you children from the family photos your grandfather sent me last year. Only you've all grown since then. I'm Mrs. Winkles. I'm so glad to finally meet you in person."

"Thank you for always remembering to send us candy for all the holidays," Jessie said after she introduced herself. "We always look forward to seeing Winkles's packages on our front porch."

"Sometimes we even open them on the front porch," Benny announced.

Mrs. Winkles chuckled. Soon she and Grandfather were busy catching up with each other while the children poked around the little shop.

"What does that say, Benny?" Soo Lee whispered. She showed Benny a sign with hearts painted all over it.

"*All Valentine's Candy Half Price*," Benny said. "I guess they're all sold out. There's nothing on the shelf."

Mrs. Winkles overheard Benny. "I usually

have some Valentine's candy left over to sell," she said. "This year, though, I had to throw out a lot of what was left over."

The children's eyes grew bigger than the foil-covered, chocolate silver dollars on the counter.

"Throw out candy?" Benny said, taken by surprise. "I never throw out candy! I save it. Then I eat it."

Mrs. Winkles smiled, but the children could tell she was thinking about something else.

"We've had one problem after another this year," Mrs. Winkles said in a hushed voice. "Lost orders, damaged shipments. So many of my customers called to complain that my Winkles Chocolate Mice arrived with pieces broken or smashed. I replaced what I could or gave people their money back. But I don't know if I'll ever get all my customers back. And I've recently had a more serious problem to deal with."

James Alden stepped closer to his friend. "The candy hearts?"

Mrs. Winkles sighed. "So you received

the hearts with the strange messages, too? Several of the stores I sell to returned their orders. Who could blame them? After all, no one wants to see a scary message on a candy heart."

"One said, *Boo!* Another one said, *Watch Out!*" Violet told Mrs. Winkles.

"Yes, I saw those," Mrs. Winkles said. "Goodness knows, I would never sell candy hearts with such messages."

Henry handed Mrs. Winkles a plastic bag. "Here are the ones we found in our boxes."

"I can't imagine how they got mixed in with mine," Mrs. Winkles said. "Everything I make or order gets packed here at my factory. Then we use a shipper to send them out. This couldn't have come at a worse time, either."

"Why is that?" Mr. Alden asked.

Mrs. Winkles looked worried. "Well, I've been hoping to supply fund-raising candy to schools that are trying to raise money. It would help my factory stay busy in between holidays. But I'll never get the school orders if there are problems with my candy."

"In kindergarten, we sell chocolate turtles," Soo Lee announced. "Then we buy swings and slides for the playground with the candy money."

Mrs. Winkles nodded. "Good for you, Soo Lee. I'm sure your school has very strict rules about the candy factories they deal with. I must have everything running exactly right when the inspectors come by."

"Have you any idea how the candy hearts with those messages got into your shipments?" James Alden asked.

Mrs. Winkles shook her head. "When we get busy before a big holiday, I hire lots of temporary help. It's impossible to track down everyone who worked here in January. Maybe someone did it as a prank."

"Not a very funny joke," James Alden said.

Henry gave this some thought. "Maybe somebody outside the factory mixed up the candy hearts."

Mrs. Winkles nodded. "I suppose that's possible. I can't bear to think anyone who works here could play such a mean trick. I haven't told anyone here about the hearts. I want to keep an eye out for anything odd going on. If the mix-up happened outside the factory, I may never figure out the mystery of how those unpleasant candies got into my shipments."

Benny couldn't stay still any longer. "We like mysteries, especially solving them. And know what else? Maybe Soo Lee and I could put the little sugar chicks inside your chocolate eggs so nobody mixes those up."

Mrs. Winkles chuckled at Benny's offer. "Thank you, Benny. But we have special machines to do that for us. I have plenty for you children to do if you want to help. Let's leave lots of time for visiting, too. I want you children to have some fun while you're here."

"What could be more fun than working in a candy factory?" Henry asked.

"When do we get to watch the candy making?" Jessie wanted to know.

"How about right now? I told my two candy makers, Meg Butterfield and Tom

Chipley, to expect you. Later on I'll show you to the guest apartment upstairs in the factory. I hope you don't mind living in the factory. You won't be able to get away from the smell of candy."

"Who would want to?" Benny asked as he followed his nose to the candy kitchen.

CHAPTER 3

A Curious Candy Tour

Mrs. Winkles locked up the candy store and led the children out into the factory area.

The Aldens breathed deeply. They couldn't get enough of the good smells of sugar, butter, chocolate, caramel, and roasting nuts.

When they reached a small room, they found white caps and aprons hanging on pegs. "You need to wear these whenever you go into the candy-making area," Mrs. Winkles said as she tucked her white curls into her white cap. "Here are some disposable gloves to wear, too. This way everything stays nice and clean."

The children giggled after they put on their white caps and aprons.

Mrs. Winkles led the Aldens into a room filled with gleaming machines, shiny copper pots, and huge silver vats. "This is the candy kitchen."

"Wow!" Benny said. "I've never been in a kitchen just for candy."

"Yoo hoo, Meg!" Mrs. Winkles called out to a woman in her early twenties across the room. She had a phone cradled on her shoulder. In front of her, a machine sprayed jets of chocolate into egg-shaped metal containers. The molds moved along on a belt just like groceries in a supermarket.

"That's our main conveyor belt," Mrs. Winkles explained. "We line up our candy molds on the conveyor belt so that they'll land right below the chocolate sprayers."

"What would happen if the molds weren't lined up right?" Benny wanted to know.

"A lot of expensive chocolate would be wasted, and there would be an awful mess to clean up," Mrs. Winkles answered. "That's why we have markings on the conveyor belt to make sure the candy molds are in the proper place. I'll have Meg or Tom show you how to do that — if Meg ever gets off the phone, that is. It's only supposed to be used for talking between the kitchen and the packing room in case someone needs to slow down the belt. Oh, I do wish Meg would do one thing at a time to cut down on mistakes."

Benny and Soo Lee couldn't believe their eyes as they watched showers of melted chocolate squirt into egg molds.

"When the molds get to the end of the line, a machine spins them to spread the chocolate evenly inside," Mrs. Winkles told the Aldens.

"Then what?" Soo Lee asked.

"After that, the molds move through a cooling tunnel," Mrs. Winkles continued, "to an area where we separate the molds from the chocolate. Then we drop in the sugar chicks. Before moving along to the packing room, the eggs get bathed in a final layer of chocolate so they're all sealed up."

"I'd like to bathe in a layer of chocolate," Henry said. "My mouth is watering."

Mrs. Winkles laughed. "Oh, you'll get so used to being around chocolate, you won't even feel like eating any at the end of the day."

"Not me!" Benny cried above the hum of the candy-making machines. "I'll never get tired of eating chocolate."

Mrs. Winkles walked the children through different small rooms in her tidy factory. "We'll see about that, Benny. When I first met my husband, I ate so much chocolate, he said I'd put him out of business. After a while, I got used to being around sweets. Eventually, I almost had to force myself to sample the candy we made to make sure it tasted right."

"Don't worry, Mrs. Winkles. You won't have to force us," Benny said. "We ate up all the Winkles Chocolate Mice you sent us even though they had no tails."

A worried look passed over Mrs. Winkles's face. "Oh, dear! You didn't tell me you received the damaged mice, too, James."

"I'm afraid so, Rose," James Alden told his old friend. "I didn't want to mention it; I was hoping it was just our shipment."

Mrs. Winkles spoke softly to the Aldens. "The problems around here began with the mice. I guess I shouldn't have put Meg in charge of so much until she had more experience. But she was highly recommended to me by a business associate she had worked for."

"That's usually the way to get good employees," Grandfather said. "Is that how you found Tom as well?"

Mrs. Winkles stopped to line up some of the egg molds that looked wobbly. "Actually, Tom practically fell out of the sky. He grew up in Ohio and trained as a banker, of all things. But he got too restless sitting behind a desk and decided to learn candy making instead. He's worked in several candy factories and knows everything about the candy business."

Benny could certainly understand wanting to be a candy maker instead of a banker. "Someday I'd like to work in candy factories. Starting now."

Mrs. Winkles forgot her worries and enjoyed Benny's funny comments. "If you keep an eye on Tom, you'll learn plenty about candy making. You'd think he grew up in a candy kitchen."

"I wish we grew up in a kitchen so we could be here all the time," Benny said.

"I only have Tom part-time," Mrs. Winkles told the Aldens. "I hired Meg before he arrived. I often wish Tom showed up first. As it is, I often have him teach Meg the most basic things about making candy. Her work is improving, but she needs constant supervision. Oh, Meg!" Mrs. Winkles called out again.

The young woman finally hung up the phone. Looking flustered, she quickly pushed a button. All the machines came to a sudden stop.

"Oh, dear, Meg. Do remember to slow down the machines first before turning them off," Mrs. Winkles said. "Now the chocolate in the molds may be smudged. You'll need to check them. Throw out any that aren't perfect."

The young woman sighed. "Sorry, Mrs. Winkles. I got startled seeing all these kids in the kitchen area. I'll be more careful."

"Maybe checking the eggs in the cooling room will be a good job for the Aldens," Mrs. Winkles told Meg.

"You're letting these kids help with the candy making?" Meg cried. "I can manage it."

"These children are old friends and careful workers," Mrs. Winkles said firmly. "There are quite a few small jobs they can do so that you won't feel rushed. This is James Alden and his grandchildren."

The children put out their hands to shake Meg's hand.

That's when Jessie noticed something.

DANGER
BE CAREFUL
WHEN BELT IS
IN MOTION

"Hi, Meg. I'm Jessie. Glad to meet you. Is it okay for us to take off our gloves, too, in this part of the candy kitchen?"

Instantly, Meg Butterfield found her disposable gloves on the counter. "Oh, I didn't realize I'd taken them off while I was on the phone."

Now Mrs. Winkles looked quite upset. "Meg! Wearing gloves is one of our most important rules. We're going to have a surprise visit from the school inspector to see if they'll hire us to make their fund-raising candy. If he sees anyone in here without gloves, we certainly won't get the job."

Meg's face grew pink under her white cap. "Sorry."

Mrs. Winkles heard the door open. "Oh, good, there's Tom. I'll have him review the candy-making steps again while the Aldens are here. I can't afford to have any more problems."

Soon, a tall, smiling man, dressed all in white just like everyone else, showed up. "Afternoon, Mrs. Winkles. Hi, Meg. Now who are these visitors? Some new customers who couldn't wait for our chocolate eggs to leave the factory? Well, I can't blame them."

Mrs. Winkles seemed more relaxed after Tom Chipley introduced himself to everyone. "Tom helps us out whenever we need him. I know he'll teach you Aldens a great deal."

"We know how to eat candy but not how to make it," Benny told Tom. "Except for fudge. We make that in our kitchen."

"But Mrs. Winkles," Meg interrupted. "I don't see why I can't handle the candy making on my own. That way you wouldn't have to waste Tom's time."

"Nonsense," Mrs. Winkles told Meg. "You'll get much more done with Tom here. That way, if we run into any problems, we can fix them right away."

"If you mean the missing tails on the mice," Meg said, "that wasn't my fault. It probably happened after the candy left the factory."

Mrs. Winkles was almost out of patience with Meg. "Well, I'm going off to a food show with Mr. Alden for a few days. I expect you to arrange a time for Tom to work with you on the production line for the next batch of chocolate eggs."

Meg looked down at the floor. "Okay," she said quietly.

Mrs. Winkles turned back to the Aldens. "Now it's time for you to attend the Winkles Candy School. I know you're on school vacation," she said, "but I hope you don't mind a class in candy making."

"Sure," Henry said. "For once, I hope we get lots of homework."

CHAPTER 4

The Aldens Go to Candy School

After Mrs. Winkles left with Grandfather, the children got down to candy business. They wanted to learn everything they could. They huddled close to Tom. He showed them everything from making chocolate to packing the cooled eggs into special Winkles egg cartons. Meg stood apart from everyone. Even the Aldens' smiles didn't make her any friendlier.

"First things first," Tom said as if he had a big secret to tell the Aldens. "I know in real school no candy is allowed in the class-room. Here at the Winkles Candy School, it's just the opposite. If you don't eat candy, we keep you after school."

"Know what?" Benny asked. "At home, Mrs. McGregor makes us wash our hands. Sometimes we even wear aprons if we're cooking."

Tom laughed. "Same here, plus gloves."

"And," Benny began, "Mrs. Winkles said we have to make sure those egg shapes are lined up right, or else the chocolate flies all over the place and makes a big mess."

"We're pretty careful around here so that doesn't happen," Meg interrupted.

Tom looked over at Meg. He seemed as if he were about to say something but changed his mind. "Over this way," he told everyone. "I'll show you the next room where we'll be working today. Mrs. Win-kles mentioned some of the chocolate eggs might have gotten smudged when the ma-chine stopped too fast."

The Aldens noticed Meg's lips tighten. "If you think it's my fault, Tom, just remember sometimes the machines cause the candy to get smudgy."

Except for the hum of the machine that kept the room cool, the room was quiet for a few seconds.

"That's not what I meant, Meg," Tom said quietly. "It could happen to anyone. First thing we do is carefully pull apart the halves of the molds by hand. If the eggs are good, we put them back on the belt so the machine can drop in the sugar chicks or whatever special candies go inside. For Halloween, we put candy ghosts inside chocolate pumpkins. For Valentine's, candy hearts go inside hollow chocolate hearts."

"Who gets to put in the chicks or ghosts or candy hearts?" Henry asked.

The children studied Tom's and Meg's faces closely. Were they going to get nervous talking about the candy hearts?

"Sometimes Meg, sometimes me," Tom said. He didn't seem at all suspicious about Henry's question or the five pairs of staring eyes.

Meg just looked bored and impatient.

"How do you keep the chicks from falling out?" Soo Lee wanted to know.

"The eggs get another chocolate bath that seals them up," Meg said a bit impatiently. "Mrs. Winkles already explained everything. Really, Tom, I don't see why we have to go over all this when there's so much to do."

After being in the warm candy kitchen, the children noticed the drop in temperature when they stepped into a cooler room. Several candy molds had already passed through the cooling tunnel. Tom pressed a switch, and the conveyor belt stopped.

"Now, pulling away the candy molds from the eggs," Tom said, "that's a job for someone with delicate, steady hands."

"That would be Violet," Jessie said. "She paints and sews and bakes perfect cakes and cookies."

"I was a baker once where I grew up in Lititz," Tom told the Aldens. "That's not far from here. Baking isn't all that different from making candy, if you think about it."

"Mrs. Winkles said you worked at a bank

in Ohio before you became a candy maker," Meg broke in.

Tom's whole face grew red. "I . . . uh . . . meant banker, not baker. I . . . did learn some baking and candy making in Lititz before I came here to get more experience. There are lots of candy factories and bakeries around that area."

The Aldens looked at each other. They were pretty sure Tom had said he was a baker not a banker, too. And Mrs. Winkles had definitely said Tom was from Ohio. Lititz was in Pennsylvania, not Ohio.

Meg stared hard at Tom. "Lititz is where Seth Winkles's relatives settled after he died. They moved from this area after he left the factory to Mrs. Winkles instead of them. Did you know they don't even speak to her anymore?"

Tom was the one not smiling now — or speaking, either. He turned away from Meg toward the children. After a few moments, he cleared his throat and spoke to the Aldens again. "Well, it's time to end Meg's history lesson and start the candy lesson," he said.

Tom wrapped his fingers around both sides of an egg mold and gently pulled apart the metal halves, which were held together by magnets. "Here's how to separate the molds."

Benny licked his lips as he saw the delicately shaped chocolate eggs when the molds were pulled apart. "Yum."

"Well, you can't eat those," Meg said. "The good ones go back on the conveyor belt to be filled. I've had this lesson more than once, Tom. I'm going back to the candy kitchen to mix up some more chocolate."

After Meg left, Tom supervised the Aldens while they removed the candy molds and checked the eggs. He was quiet now, not teasing or joking with the Aldens anymore.

"Where do the smudgy ones go?" Jessie asked after she found some eggs with blurry designs.

Tom didn't answer, so Jessie spoke up again. "Where do the —"

"I heard you the first time," Tom answered. "I just need to concentrate on this batch. Put them in that big plastic bin. Take what you want. Doesn't matter to me."

"Are you sure?" Benny asked.

"I wouldn't have said it if I wasn't sure. I'm going to get the chick machine going now — make sure it's running, and all," Tom explained. "We won't be able to fill very many more chocolate eggs. We only have a few candy chicks left right now. I'm picking up a new shipment tomorrow."

While Tom checked the machine to see how it was working, the Aldens were working, too. They had steady fingers and good eyes. In no time, they could tell right away if an egg was perfect or not. Luckily, most of them were.

"Hey, Tom!" Henry called out when the children were done. "Can we really eat all the smudged ones like you said? It's getting hard to look at all this chocolate and not have some."

Tom didn't seem to hear Henry.

"Is that machine working okay?" Jessie hoped Tom would look up from whatever he was doing. "All these eggs are ready to be filled."

Tom looked up when he heard the Aldens coming his way.

"Is the machine okay?" Jessie asked again.

"Yeah, yeah," Tom answered. "No problem. Listen, just take those rejected eggs home to eat, okay? I'll see you tomorrow."

The Aldens didn't move right away. Now that their work was done, they wanted to share their candy with Tom.

"Go on, now," Tom said. "I've got everything under control."

Henry took the candy bin outside. He set it down on the steps where the children could sit and have their sweets. "What happened with Tom in there? One minute he was all friendly," Henry said. "Then he acted as if he wanted us to go away."

"I know," Jessie said, not a bit hungry for chocolate anymore. "It seemed to have

something to do with whatever Meg said. I was confused."

Benny wasn't quite as hungry as he'd been earlier, but he wasn't going to let all this chocolate go to waste. He broke off piece after piece of the chocolate eggs. "I'd rather be a baker than a banker any day," he said. "But most of all, I want to be a candy maker like Tom."

"He sure is good at his job, for someone who learned it kind of late," Jessie noted.

"Maybe he's a fast learner," Benny said. "Like me."

CHAPTER 5

A Candy Mix-up

After dinner that night, the children unpacked their things. The cozy loft apartment on the top floor of the candy factory was just the right size for the five Aldens. It had a living area and kitchen on one side and a sleeping area with several cots on the other.

When Jessie opened the cabinets, she was pleased to see a set of red and white dishes and pots and pans inside. "We'll be able to make our own meals when we want to."

Benny flopped down on the couch and

held his stomach. "You won't have to make any meals for me ever again."

The Aldens had never heard Benny say *that* before!

"What's the matter, Benny?" Henry asked.

"I shouldn't have eaten all those broken chocolate egg pieces. Now I'm turning into chocolate."

Henry laughed. "I thought you wanted to live in the candy factory. That's why Mrs. Winkles let us stay in this loft instead of at her house."

"Here, have some of this ginger ale that Mrs. McGregor put in the cooler," Jessie suggested. "That sometimes settles down stomachaches."

Benny sat up and took a few fizzy sips. "I feel a little better."

"Good," Jessie said. "From now on, let's make sure we don't take so many samples even if Tom says it's okay. We'll mainly be working with Meg tomorrow anyway. That's what Mrs. Winkles said."

The other children frowned when they heard this.

"Even though Tom wasn't so friendly when we left," Violet began, "I'd still rather work with him than with Meg. I don't think she wants us around."

Jessie found some blankets in a chest and lay one on each cot. "It's probably my fault for asking about her work gloves. I didn't mean to get her in trouble with Mrs. Winkles."

"Well, tomorrow we can get a fresh start now that Tom showed us what to do," Henry said. "He seems to know a lot about making candy. Now we know a little bit, too."

"Like not eating too much candy while we work," Benny said before he finally fell asleep.

By the next morning, Benny's stomachache was gone. "I could even eat chocolate chip pancakes," he announced happily.

"Maybe you could," Jessie told Benny. "But Henry and I made fruit salad from the fruit Mrs. McGregor sent along with us. We'll have it with nice, healthy cereal. No chocolate chip pancakes today."

Benny wasn't too disappointed. After all, he was living in a candy factory. He could get sweets anytime he wanted. He went over to Violet and Soo Lee, who were still sleeping. He tickled their feet.

"Stop it, Watch!" Violet said before opening her eyes. "It's too early."

Soo Lee giggled. "That's not Watch. It's Benny."

Soon, the whole family was up and about, eager to begin the day. After Jessie and Henry's good breakfast, everyone helped tidy up the loft.

Henry went over by the window to hang up the dish towel. That's when he noticed someone down in the parking lot below. "Looks as if we're not the only early birds. Tom's down there." Henry opened the window. "Hey, Tom," he yelled. "We're up here!"

By this time, the other children crowded at the window to wave to Tom, too.

"We'll be right down!" Jessie yelled. Then she said to the other children, "That's funny. Why is he getting in his car?"

Violet looked puzzled. "He didn't wave or say hi. Don't you think he saw us or heard us?"

"Maybe he forgot something at home and had to run back for it," Henry said. "Oh, well, we'd better go downstairs. I'd like to get organized before Meg gets to work. I don't want her saying we're late or anything."

Jessie checked the kitchen clock. "It's not even seven o'clock. I wonder why Tom got to work so early. Well, let's go. Mrs. Winkles told Tom and Meg to leave a key for us in the candy shop window box. She said we could go into the candy-making area that way."

A few minutes later, the children found the key in the window box. Everyone huddled around Jessie as she fiddled with the lock.

"It doesn't fit," Jessie said, trying the key one way, then the other. "I wonder if this is the right key. Let's go around back and see if it works on one of the other doors."

Jessie tried out the key on several

doors. The children could see right away that their small key didn't fit the big factory lock.

"Let's go back upstairs and call Tom or Meg to see when they're coming in," Jessie suggested.

Henry called Tom's number first when the children went back to the loft. "Hi, Tom," he said when someone picked up. "It's Henry. We're locked . . . Hey, don't hang up." Henry put down the phone. "I must have dialed the wrong number. I thought it sort of sounded like Tom, but then the person hung up."

Henry tried again, dialing more carefully this time. "That was Tom's answering machine," Henry said when he hung up. "I'll try Meg. Does anybody have her phone number?"

No one did.

"You know what," Jessie said. "Since we have to wait for Tom and Meg anyway, why don't we do our grocery shopping now for our lunch? Mrs. Winkles mentioned a store not too far from here that opens early.

Maybe by the time we come back, Tom and Meg will be here."

Violet started a shopping list. "What do we need?"

"Not candy!" Soo Lee and Benny cried out together.

By the time the Aldens returned from the store and put their groceries away, Meg's car was in the parking lot.

"That's funny," Jessie said when everyone discovered the candy kitchen was still locked. "I hear the candy machines humming inside. I wonder why Meg didn't unlock this."

Henry banged on the big metal door as loud as he could.

"We're locked out," Henry yelled. Finally, the door opened. Meg stood there and stared at the Aldens. "I can't just stop the candy making to open doors and such," she said. "Well, go get dressed as long as you're here."

Jessie showed Meg the key that didn't fit. "This is the wrong key."

Meg stared at it. "Oh, that's a key for one of the storage areas. Sorry. I must have left it out by mistake. Well, it doesn't matter. Just go to the changing room to get your caps and aprons."

After the children put on caps, gloves, and white aprons, they stepped into the candy kitchen. Right away, they noticed some chocolate egg molds moving along the conveyor belt. No one seemed to be watching them.

"What's the matter now?" Meg asked.

Jessie pointed to the machinery. "Isn't someone supposed to supervise the conveyor belt when it's on?"

Meg didn't appreciate the reminder about this. "Never mind. Just go to the other room. Make sure the eggs I made yesterday all have sugar chicks in them. Then start packing the eggs into the egg cartons the way Tom showed you. And don't break any."

The Aldens were glad to begin work away from Meg.

"Remember what Mrs. Winkles said,"

Jessie reminded everyone. "Make sure all the eggs are smooth and completely sealed up before you put them into the egg cartons."

"I know, I know," Soo Lee said. "And make sure that we can hear a little chickie inside each one. We have to pick the eggs up softly to make sure the chick is in there."

Pretty soon the Aldens were hard at work. Only checking and packing the beautiful chocolate eggs into cartons didn't seem a bit like work.

"Do we get to keep the ones that don't have a chick inside?" Benny asked after several of his eggs sounded empty. "Don't worry. I won't eat too much chocolate today. I promise."

After a while, the Aldens had a pile of cartons ready for shipping. But they also had a pile of empty eggs, too.

"Uh-oh," Henry said. "I hate to say it, but look how many eggs went through without any chicks inside." He walked over to the phone on the wall. "The red phone light is on. Meg must be using it. Let's go tell her the machine missed a bunch. Violet can stay here with Soo Lee and Benny to finish up."

Jessie frowned. "This is terrible. Mrs. Winkles loses money when she has to throw out the imperfect eggs."

When Henry and Jessie joined Meg, she was still using the phone.

"No wonder there are always problems," Jessie whispered to Henry. "She doesn't seem to pay attention to what she's doing."

The two children caught the last few words of Meg's conversation. "I have to go, Mr. Boxer. I can't keep talking to you so much. I have a lot of work to do."

"Now what?" Meg asked Henry and Jessie. She reached over to turn off the machine. "Whenever you leave the packing or cooling rooms, you're supposed to call me to slow down the machine so there's no pileup."

Jessie stepped forward. "Violet, Benny, and Soo Lee are still working in there. We tried to call, but the line was busy. So we came over instead."

"A whole bunch of eggs came through without any chicks inside," Henry said. "Something must be wrong with the machine." He went over to check it.

Jessie looked upset. "Maybe when Tom gets back we can figure out a solution."

"We don't need Tom today," Meg told the Aldens. "Get away from that machine, Henry. Go finish packing the rest of the eggs."

Meg came over to the chick machine and looked underneath it. "This part jammed up the opening. That's why the chicks didn't drop down. Did you do something to this just now or when you were working with Tom yesterday?"

Henry shook his head. "I never touched it."

"Well, somebody must have done something," Meg said, her voice shaking. "I can't get it going at all now."

"Maybe Tom can help," Jessie suggested. "In fact, he was already here this morning. He's probably on an errand and coming back."

Meg's eyebrows shot up. "Tom was here already? So I guess he was the one who left the lights on. I'm always getting blamed for every little thing that goes wrong. Mrs. Winkles thinks he never makes mistakes, but he even forgot to lock the door. That's why I locked it after I got inside, so I wouldn't forget. Well, I guess I have no choice but to call him."

"Good luck reaching him," Henry said. "I thought he answered the phone. But after the line got disconnected and I redialed, all I got was his answering machine. Wherever he went, it wasn't back home. I don't know where he is."

"Probably making more problems," Meg muttered, "instead of helping me out."

CHAPTER 6

Broken Eggs

When Meg still couldn't get the sugar chick machine going, she sent the Aldens home for an early lunch. "I'll call you when Tom arrives," she told the children. "I left a message for him to come in and fix the machine."

"And we can fix lunch!" Benny announced.

When the children returned to the loft, Benny and Violet headed straight for the refrigerator. They lined up all the lunch fixings on the kitchen counter, just like a conveyor belt.

"This is the Alden Tuna Fish Factory," Benny said. "First, Soo Lee puts lettuce on the bread then slides it to me. Then I plop the tuna on the lettuce and slide the bread to Violet. She cuts the sandwiches and adds pickles. Then we do the next sandwich and the next one and the next one."

Jessie and Henry got a kick out of Benny's system.

"You don't even need a machine, either," Henry said. "Boy, was Meg ever upset about that broken machine! I hope it gets fixed soon so Mrs. Winkles doesn't lose any more business."

The phone rang just as Violet passed around the sandwich plates. "That's probably Meg calling to tell us when to come back."

Jessie picked it up. "Oh, hi, Mrs. Winkles. We thought it was Meg. Yes, we're on our lunch break." Jessie paused. "Oh, so Meg told you about the problem with the chick machine? Sure, we can bring the part to get fixed." Jessie grabbed a pencil and paper. "Just give me the address. We'll go to the repair place this afternoon. I'll put on Benny and Soo Lee so Grandfather can talk to them."

As the younger children chatted on the phone with James Alden, Jessie explained what Mrs. Winkles wanted the children to do. "She gave me the name of the tool-maker who takes care of the candy machines. She said Tom took the part in to get it fixed a couple of times before. She couldn't believe that it was broken again."

Violet looked thoughtful. "Was Mrs. Winkles upset?"

"A little," Jessie answered. "Here's the strange thing. She spoke to Tom, and he made it sound as if there was a problem with the machine when he showed it to us yesterday — that it broke while we were working with him."

"But that's not true!" Henry said. "Besides, how could Tom know about the part being broken? He wasn't even there when Meg got to work this morning."

Jessie frowned. "And when he was here this morning, he acted as if he didn't want to see us."

After the Aldens finished lunch, they went to get the broken part from Meg. They heard her voice coming from Mrs. Winkles's office.

"Mr. Boxer, you really shouldn't be in here," the Aldens overheard Meg say to someone else in the office. "I was just locking up."

"After all, Meg, I am Mrs. Winkles's shipper," the man said. "I just need to check some old shipping bills. I'll only be a few minutes."

Meg sounded a little worried. "But why are you looking at— "

"Oh, never mind," the man said impatiently. "Since you and I worked together, Meg, I'm really not sure why you're such a fussbudget about my being here. Remember, I did help you get this job. We're supposed to be helping each other."

Meg noticed the Aldens standing nearby. For a change, she seemed relieved to see them. "Oh, I'm glad you're all here. I have that broken machine part Mrs. Winkles called about," she said. "This is Mr. Boxer. He's my old boss from the shipping company where I used to work. He ships all our packages."

The man didn't seem a bit interested in meeting the Aldens. He barely turned around from the file cabinet he was trying to open. "Humph," was his way of saying hello. "It's no use," he muttered. "It's locked." With that, he brushed by the Aldens without another word.

The children still didn't feel comfortable around Meg. But now she looked so worried, they almost felt sorry for her.

"What's the matter?" Violet asked.

"Oh, nothing," Meg said softly. She gathered up all the papers the man had scattered on Mrs. Winkles's desk.

"I bet Mrs. Winkles is a nicer boss than that man was," Benny told Meg.

"Benny," Jessie whispered. "That's not our business."

Meg started to say something else but

stopped. Finally, she held out the broken machine part. "Here it is. Don't forget to tell them that we need it fixed as soon as possible. I'll see you later."

When the children turned to leave, Tom appeared in front of them as if he had come out of nowhere.

"Tom!" Jessie said. "We were waiting for you to come back."

Tom looked away from the Aldens. "What do you mean, come back? I just got here."

Jessie scrunched her eyebrows. What did Tom mean by that? "Weren't you here really early this morning? We saw you in the parking lot. We all waved down at you."

Tom waited a long time before speaking. "Wasn't me. You must have seen someone else. I was home all morning."

Now Henry was confused, too. "But I called you there. Your answering machine was on."

"I must have been in the shower," Tom said.

"Guess what," Soo Lee said, looking up at Tom. "Mrs. Winkles's chick machine broke. We're getting it fixed."

Now it was Tom's turn to look startled. "That's why I came by. Mrs. Winkles also left a message on my machine. I'm the one who goes to the toolmaker's to make sure he does the job right. It's not an errand for kids."

Jessie looked up at Tom. "Mrs. Winkles told us to go," she said in a firm voice. "We just talked to her. See you later." Jessie led the children out before Tom could say another word.

The Aldens didn't have to go far to find the tool repair shop. It was just a few blocks away.

Jessie looked down at the scrap of paper with the toolmaker's address on it. "There's the place—*All-Tool Casting*. Let's see if they can help us."

The children entered the small shop, which was filled with all kinds of metal parts.

A man in blue overalls came out to greet the Aldens. "May I help you?"

Jessie put the broken machine part on the counter. "We're from the Winkles Candy Factory. Mrs. Winkles asked us to get this fixed."

"Her candy chick machine broke again," Soo Lee told the man.

"That sounds like an emergency," the man said with a friendly twinkle in his eye.

"It is an emergency!" Benny said. "A candy emergency. But Mrs. Winkles said you fixed it before when Tom came here. Now it's broken again."

"Before?" the man asked in a puzzled voice. "I haven't worked on this broken part before."

Now it was the Aldens' turn to be confused.

"Are you sure?" Henry asked. "Don't you know Tom Chipley? He works for Mrs. Winkles sometimes. He told her he's been in here a few times with this broken part."

"Never met him," the man said. He could see Benny on his tiptoes, trying to see all the machines in the back of his shop. "I am glad to meet you kids, though. Sorry I can't let you back there — safety and all, you know. I make machine parts for candy machines plus candy molds and design stamps for a lot of the candy factories in the area. There's a lot of stuff back there that could be dangerous for kids."

The man took a close look at the broken machine part. "Hmmm, I see the problem here. I can have it ready day after tomorrow. Hope that's okay."

"It'll have to be," Henry said. "Thanks for getting it done so quickly."

"See you in a couple days," the man said. "Oh, help yourself to some candy from that basket over by those packages on the counter. I get lots of free samples from my customers who order parts for their candy-making equipment."

Benny and Soo Lee didn't need to be coaxed to help themselves. Benny reached in and grabbed a handful. He recited the names of all the candy he wanted to try: "Taffy Pulls, Choco Chewies, *Stay Out!*"

"Stay out of where?" Henry asked. "What are you talking about?"

Benny held up a candy heart. "That's what it says. It's like one of the hearts Mrs. Winkles gave us."

While the children were talking, a man in a brown uniform pushed a hand truck into the shop. "Hi, kids. I see you found the free candy they keep around here. This is one of my favorite stops."

When the deliveryman went over to the counter to pick up a pile of boxes, Henry followed him. "I'll give you a hand. There are an awful lot of packages."

"Thanks," the man said. "I can't let you handle the packages. But you can hold my hand truck steady while I pile the shipments on it. Let's see." The man began to read the labels: "*Sturgis, Wilber, Boxer.*"

"*Boxer!*" the Aldens all cried at the same time.

"I sure don't want to forget this one," the deliveryman said. "He's a tough customer. And he got me in some trouble with a few of my customers. Blamed me for mixing up some of my deliveries." The man stopped. "I can't really discuss this. Let's just say there have been a few mix-ups with that guy."

"Candy mix-ups?" Jessie asked.

The man pushed his hand truck out the door. "I guess you could say that."

CHAPTER 7

The Aldens See a Ghost

The next morning, the Aldens had no problem getting into the candy kitchen. Meg had left a message in big letters on the Aldens' door the night before: *Get to work early. We need everybody to help fill the eggs by hand.*

"How long did you say it would take to fix the part?" Meg asked again as she let the children inside. "Mrs. Winkles called a few times to make sure I'm keeping up the work."

"The tool man said a couple of days,"

Jessie answered Meg. "I guess it's good that we came to visit Mrs. Winkles. Now you'll have lots of helpers until the machine gets fixed."

Meg wasn't quite so sure of that. "It doesn't matter how many people you have. Doing things by hand is always slower. I guess it's better than nothing. I want to show Mrs. Winkles I can manage the candy factory even when she's not here."

Meg led the children past the first cooling room where the sugar chick machine was usually running. "Tom offered to pick up two containers of sugar chicks from Mr. Boxer's. He didn't want to lose time waiting for Mr. Boxer to deliver them."

Benny and Soo Lee looked with big eyes at the huge, plastic jars filled with blue and yellow candies.

"Anyway, the containers are opened already. You can just start dropping the chicks into the eggs," Meg continued. "I'll run the conveyor belt at the slowest speed. Be very careful."

Jessie nodded. "We'll be extra careful. I know we can work fast and not make mistakes."

Meg's cheeks grew pink. "What is that supposed to mean? That I make mistakes and you don't?"

Jessie swallowed hard. "No, no. I didn't mean it that way — just that everybody makes mistakes."

"She's so touchy," Henry whispered after Meg finally left.

"And a little careless," Jessie added. "But at least that would be better than if she's harming Mrs. Winkles's business on purpose."

The Aldens weren't at all careless when it came to work. They lined themselves up in a row to make sure that if one person missed an egg, someone else filled it.

"Okay, everybody. Ready?" Henry asked.

A soft hum filled the spotless white room. Slowly the conveyor belt began to move a row of chocolate eggs through an opening in the wall, toward the Aldens.

"Here goes." Henry reached into the metal container of candy chicks and took one out. "I'll start."

Filling the eggs was simple, but Henry did miss a few at first. Jessie and Violet caught them all.

"Do Soo Lee and I get a turn?" Benny asked.

"Sure," Henry said. "Now that we've got a good system going, you and Soo Lee scoot in front of me and you fill them, okay?"

This worked so well that the children were ahead of the machine every few minutes.

Then Benny's sharp eyes spotted something different when he reached into the container. Instead of a sugar chick, he saw a ghost instead! "Look at this. It's a candy ghost, not a chick!"

Violet recognized the little white ghosts. "Those are the ghosts Mrs. Winkles puts in her chocolate Halloween pumpkins. How did they get mixed up with the chicks?"

Henry saw that a couple empty eggs were

about to pass by Benny. "I don't know, but I'm glad Benny has a good eye for candy. Set it aside for now. I'll fill these two eggs."

"Let's not talk until the conveyor belt stops," Jessie said. "The last thing we need is to get distracted. It's bad enough that Meg doesn't pay attention to her job half the time. Now this. I don't think customers would like seeing a ghost inside a chocolate egg when it isn't Halloween."

"Hey, everything is slowing down," Soo Lee noticed a few minutes later. "See, it stopped."

"Before Meg comes in here or calls us, let's check these containers real fast," Jessie suggested. "We'd better find out if any other candy ghosts got mixed in."

The children sorted through the containers. They found a dozen or so candy ghosts in each one.

"Should we tell Meg?" Violet asked.

Henry and Jessie looked at each other.

"Not yet," Henry said. "First, we need to find out who did this. Don't forget, when she gave us these containers, they were already opened. Let's just keep an eye on her for now."

Violet didn't like to think that people they knew would make any trouble. "Maybe Meg opened the containers but didn't know what was inside."

"I hate to say this, but what about Tom?" Henry asked. "He said he wasn't anywhere near the factory this morning, but we saw him. He's also the one who gave Meg the candy chick containers."

Benny looked a little upset. "He didn't wave at us the other morning."

Jessie put her arm around Benny and smiled. "Well, it's not a crime not to wave at people, Benny."

"I know," Benny said. "But first he was nice and gave everybody candy and showed us stuff. Then he stopped being so nice."

A ringing phone interrupted the children.

"Meg said the inspector just drove up," Jessie told the others after she picked up the phone. "She needs us to come to the candy kitchen. Hurry!"

"I wonder why Meg couldn't just let the

inspector in to see us working," Henry said as the children rushed to see what Meg was so upset about. "Isn't the whole idea of a surprise visit to check that the candy factory is okay no matter when somebody shows up? Uh-oh."

When the Aldens stepped into the candy kitchen, it was not okay, not at all. Meg was racing from one end of the room to the other with paper wipes and sponges.

"What happened?" Jessie asked when she saw a pool of chocolate spreading over the conveyor belt.

Meg pointed to the controls on the chocolate sprayers. "Turn them off! Hurry! I have to let the inspector in. He just rang the bell. You clean up the mess. I'll see if I can keep him from coming in here until we get this under control. I'll slow him down while he's getting dressed to come in here."

After Meg left, the Aldens raced into action. Jessie and Henry found the clean paper wipes Tom had told them to use for any spills. Jessie mixed up a pan of warm, soapy water for the final cleanup.

Violet was the one who noticed what had caused the chocolate sprays to miss the molds. "They weren't lined up right. When the chocolate sprayed, it missed part of the last few molds. See?"

After Henry and Jessie had completely wiped down the conveyor belt, the other children lined up clean molds exactly under the sprayers.

"There," Jessie said. She did a quick check of the area to make sure that no chocolate had spilled off the belt onto the floor.

But before she finished, the inspector stepped into the room. "So this is where you make the candy?" The man stood in the doorway looking over the candy kitchen as if he were inspecting a hospital.

That's when Jessie noticed something terrible. Meg wasn't wearing her gloves! She tried to get Meg's attention by holding up her hands when the inspector was checking behind boxes of cooking chocolate.

Meg didn't seem to know what Jessie was trying to tell her. Instead, she moved around the candy kitchen like a nervous mouse in a cage. "Here are the pots of warm chocolate," Meg told the man. "This is where we pour the chocolate into the molds."

"You don't have to explain the process," the inspector said. "It's my job to know these things. I just have to make sure everything is completely . . ." The inspector froze in place, then pointed to Meg's hands. "Where are your gloves, Miss?"

Meg stared down at her hands, then quickly put them behind her back. "Uh, I took them off when I let you in. I did wash my hands while you were dressing," she said finally.

The inspector didn't say anything. He simply wrote something down in his notebook.

The Aldens couldn't believe Meg had left off her gloves again — with the inspector there, too! Was she *trying* to fail the inspection?

Meg didn't say a word as she led the inspector to the other areas of the factory.

She was so nervous, she dropped her key ring in the packing room. When she picked up her keys, she bumped into a stack of egg cartons. "Don't worry, I won't send those out," she told the inspector after he wrote something down again.

"This is a disaster. I don't see how Mrs. Winkles will pass inspection with all these mistakes," Henry whispered to Jessie when Meg and the inspector went off to the packing room by themselves.

Jessie sighed. "Sometimes she just works too fast and doesn't pay attention." Jessie pointed to a door Meg had left open. "See? She went out without closing that door."

Benny scooted over so the inspector wouldn't see the open door.

In a few minutes, Meg and the inspector rejoined the Aldens.

As everyone walked back to the candy kitchen, the inspector finally put his pen away. "I'll be making my report in a few days. I'll come back for another visit so you have a chance to fix some of the problems that came up today." As he was about to leave, the inspector froze dead in the doorway. "What is that cat doing in the candy kitchen?"

The Aldens crowded behind the man to see what he was talking about. Under the mixing counter, a cat the children had seen around the factory was enjoying a speck of chocolate the children hadn't noticed.

"Why, I never!" the inspector sputtered. "Children in the kitchen is one thing in these family businesses, but a cat?" Out came the man's pen once again.

Meg ran over to the spilled chocolate. She tried to clean it up. "Shoo! Shoo!" she yelled at the cat.

"Yeow!" the cat answered before he licked himself and strolled out the door that Meg had left open.

CHAPTER 8

Something's Cooking

When the Aldens returned to the loft, Henry made a decision. "You know," he began, "it seems as if Meg is so careless, she's hurting Mrs. Winkles's business even if she's not doing it on purpose. We've got to find out what is going on with her and with Mr. Boxer."

Jessie agreed. "She even let him into Mrs. Winkles's office. Something's going on with those two."

"Tom's the one who brought over containers of sugar chicks with the candy

ghosts mixed in," Henry reminded everyone. "Maybe he mixed up the candies before he gave them to Meg."

"I don't like to think anything bad about
Tom," Violet said in her quiet way. "Tom
might not have known anything about the
mix-up."

Benny tapped Jessie's elbow. "Know
what? All the candy came from Mr. Boxer's
warehouse — the candy ghosts, the candy
hearts with the scary messages, even the
mice."

Henry put his hand up for a high five.
"You're right! Here's what I'm thinking.
Mrs. Winkles said we could visit the warehouse to see how they ship the candy. Let's
go now. Maybe we'll clear up a few mysteries there."

The Aldens were soon on their way to
Boxer's Shipping Company, which was
about a mile from Winkles Candy Factory.
When they arrived, the children found
more than a mystery to clear up.

"Mrs. Winkles's egg cartons — the ones

we packed. Look!" Jessie pointed to the loading platform. "Somebody just left them sitting out in the sun. I know it's cold out, but the chocolate eggs will be ruined if they stay there too long. They should be in the shade or in a cooler place."

"Why would Mr. Boxer let all of Mrs. Winkles's candy get ruined?" asked Benny.

"I don't know," said Violet, "but we better do something before this chocolate melts!"

The children noticed two men loading a truck.

"Hey, hey!" Henry yelled out when the men shoved the boxes into the truck any which way. "We're working for Mrs. Winkles. Those are her candy shipments. See, the shipping boxes say, *Handle With Care.* And there's a pile of her chocolate egg cartons just sitting in the sun. They're going to melt if someone doesn't move them to someplace cooler."

The two men looked at each other. Who was the teenage boy telling them how to do their job?

"The boss says we have to get this truck loaded in a hurry," one of the men told the Aldens. "He told us to leave those boxes over there. He must know what he's doing."

"That's what we're afraid of," Jessie whispered to Henry. She looked up at the men. "Could we at least get them out of the sun? We'll move them for you if that's okay."

"You kids are from Winkles?" one of the men said, looking over the Aldens. "Well, check with the boss. He's inside. If he says it's okay, then it's okay."

The children climbed the steps to the loading platform. As soon as Henry pushed the door that led inside, the children all sniffed the air at the same time.

"Chocolate!" Soo Lee said. "It smells just like Winkles Candy Factory."

"The smell seems to be coming from over there." Henry pointed to a door at the far end of the warehouse.

The children began to make their way to the back, then stopped. They heard a door slam behind them. The sound of heavy footsteps came closer.

Mr. Boxer stood directly behind them. "Stay right there," he ordered. He stepped around the children, then marched to the back of the warehouse. He shut the door and cut off the sweet candy smells flowing through the warehouse.

The Aldens didn't move.

"Who let you in here?" Mr. Boxer's question boomed through the warehouse. "You're those kids I saw the other day. What are you doing here?"

Henry was about to answer when Mr. Boxer's phone rang.

Mr. Boxer waved away the children. "Go back outside. I'll be out in a few minutes. I need to answer this."

The Aldens obeyed Mr. Boxer. On their way out, they caught a few snatches of Mr. Boxer's conversation. "Did you send those kids here . . . ?" The words trailed off before the children could tell who was at the other end of the phone.

"Was that Mrs. Winkles?" Jessie asked in

a friendly voice when Mr. Boxer returned a few minutes later. "Or Meg?"

Mr. Boxer stared at Jessie. "That was . . . um . . . just a business call. And speaking of that, what business do you kids have coming into my warehouse? I can't have people just roaming around inside or even out here. You could fall off the loading dock. Then where would you be?"

"On the ground?" Soo Lee looked up at Mr. Boxer.

Mr. Boxer didn't find this funny. "If Rose Winkles sent you here, go back and tell her I can't get her candy shipped out with a bunch of kids underfoot."

"But the candy was in the sun," Benny said. "It could melt and get squished like Mrs. Winkles's — "

Henry nudged Benny so he wouldn't say anything else.

"Look here," Mr. Boxer broke in. "I ship candy for a lot of companies. I don't need to be told how to do my job. Now you kids can just get out of here." Mr. Boxer suddenly looked over the Aldens' heads.

The children turned around to look behind them. They saw a car drive around the side of the warehouse.

"Get going now," Mr. Boxer told the Aldens, this time more firmly than before. "I have an important visitor."

"I know one thing," Henry muttered after Mr. Boxer left. "He sure doesn't want us snooping around."

"And I know one other thing," Jessie added. "When somebody doesn't want us snooping around, there's usually a reason."

"Can Soo Lee and I run in back of the warehouse to see who just drove in?" Benny asked.

Jessie nodded. "Well, okay, Benny, but just for a minute. Take a quick peek, then catch up with us right away. I don't want to hear any more of Mr. Boxer's orders."

Benny grabbed Soo Lee's hand and disappeared around the side of the warehouse. The older children strolled slowly toward the street. A couple of minutes later, the younger children returned.

Benny was out of breath. He took a few

gulps of air. "Guess what. The man . . ." Benny could hardly get the words out. "The man who came to Mrs. Winkles's factory and checked everything, that's who's visiting Mr. Boxer. They went into a little building that's part of the warehouse. That's where the candy smells are coming from. We could smell candy, but we couldn't see it."

"You mean the inspector?" Violet asked. "Why would he be here?"

"Oh, I suppose that's not so strange," Jessie said. "He probably has to make sure the candy doesn't get spoiled or anything before it gets shipped."

"Then why did they meet in back?" Henry pointed out. "All the shipments are in front on the loading dock and in the truck."

"From what Benny and Soo Lee saw, it sounds as if Mr. Boxer is making candy," Violet said. "He could be trying to get the school candy business for himself."

"You know what else?" Jessie asked. "I think Mr. Boxer planted his own spy at Mrs. Winkles's factory — either Meg or Tom.

After all, Meg used to work for him. As for Tom, well, even Mrs. Winkles said he practically dropped out of the sky. Let's tell the two of them that we saw Mr. Boxer's place and see what they have to say."

"Or not say," Henry added.

CHAPTER 9

Something Sweet, Something Fishy

The children had a lot to talk about. As they crossed the parking lot to return to the loft, the inspector's car passed by and drove away.

"I guess he's all done here," Henry said. "I'd sure like to know why he stopped by. Look, Mr. Boxer is leaving, too."

The Aldens waved at Mr. Boxer when his van went by, but he didn't wave back.

"What are you smiling about, Jessie?" Violet asked when she noticed a grin on her sister's face. "Mr. Boxer didn't look very friendly just now."

Jessie went on grinning. "I left my sweater in the warehouse."

Now the other children looked just as confused as Violet.

"That's nothing to smile about," Henry said.

"Yes, it is," Jessie replied. "I left it behind on purpose. Now that Mr. Boxer is gone, we have an excuse to go back inside to get it. Only let's go the back way where Benny and Soo Lee were."

"Good plan, Jessie," Henry said. "What are we waiting for?"

Jessie quickly ran ahead to find her sweater. When she came out, the other Aldens were waiting in front of a small building. It looked a lot newer than the rest of the warehouse.

The children breathed in the sweet, sugary air.

"Somebody was definitely cooking candy or something sweet in there," Violet said.

Benny and Soo Lee crept up to the building first. A window was opened slightly, but they weren't tall enough to see in.

Henry was. "Hey, guys. Take a look inside!"

Violet and Jessie stood behind Henry. He picked up Benny, and Jessie picked up Soo Lee. Now the two younger Aldens could see a gleaming candy kitchen. It was newer and smaller than Mrs. Winkles's kitchen, but equipped with the same kinds of pots and candy molds.

"So Mr. Boxer is a candy maker, not just a shipper," Jessie said. "Now that's pretty fishy. I don't think Mrs. Winkles knows about this. She might not want to use a shipper who's competing with her."

Violet looked worried. "If Mr. Boxer is making candy, too, that would explain why he's not careful about Mrs. Winkles's candy. Maybe we should come back with Mrs. Winkles when Mr. Boxer doesn't expect us. That way she can see for herself what is going on."

"Good idea," Henry agreed. "Maybe we'll catch him in the act."

"Let's bring Tom and Meg, too," Jessie suggested. "We need to find out once and for all if they've been making trouble — and candy — with Mr. Boxer."

The children headed to the loading dock.

"Hi," Jessie said to the two workmen. "Would you give Mr. Boxer a message that we'll be back in a couple of days?"

"Okay," one of the men said.

Henry was confused. "Why did you tell them when we're coming? Wouldn't it be better to just show up and surprise them?"

A smile spread across Jessie's face. "We're not going to come by in a couple of days — we'll come back tomorrow morning. Mr. Boxer won't have a chance to hide anything suspicious."

"Now it looks as if Mr. Boxer might be causing problems for Mrs. Winkles," Violet said. "Thank goodness it's not Tom."

"I wouldn't be so sure about Tom yet," Jessie said. "We still have to find out why he tried to make Mrs. Winkles think we had something to do with the broken machine. Don't forget that. Plus, he said he wasn't in the factory the other morning when we saw him with our own eyes."

Violet bit her lip. "I know there must be a good reason for the way Tom acted. I hope we can find out about him and about Meg, too. After all, she's the one who always seems to be talking with Mr. Boxer, not Tom."

When the Aldens returned to the candy factory, they noticed Tom's and Meg's cars in the parking lot.

"We need to get everybody over to Mr. Boxer's, that's for sure," Henry said. "Mrs. Winkles and Grandfather are coming back tonight. We could tell Mrs. Winkles that we saw some problems at Mr. Boxer's warehouse."

"Good idea, Henry," Jessie agreed. "We'll ask her if she can go there to have him show us how the candy gets shipped out."

As the children walked closer to Mrs. Winkles's office, they heard angry voices.

"We'd better wait a bit," Jessie whispered. "Sounds as if Meg and Tom are having another one of their disagreements. I don't want to get caught in the middle."

"If you gave me the right directions in the first place, Tom," Meg was saying, "I wouldn't have put vanilla in the chocolate batch too early. You never said to add it at the end. I couldn't find Mrs. Winkles's recipe book anywhere to help me out."

"You've been here long enough to know the steps by now," Tom said.

Henry knocked on the office door.

When Tom turned around, the Aldens crowded into the office. "We were wondering when you were coming back," Tom said. "Not that it matters. The last batch of chocolate's no good. We have to mix up more. Where did you go?"

"To Mr. Boxer's warehouse," Henry said slowly. "Before Mrs. Winkles left, she told us we could take a look at how Mr. Boxer sends out her candy shipments."

The children were disappointed. Neither Tom nor Meg seemed to care a bit that the Aldens had visited Mr. Boxer's.

Meg seemed more interested in arguing

with Tom than talking with the Aldens. "All I need is Mrs. Winkles's recipe notebook again. If you had put it back after you borrowed it the other day, I wouldn't have made the mistake about the vanilla."

"You shouldn't need the recipe to know that the vanilla goes in last," Tom said.

At that moment, Meg happened to look down at Tom's open briefcase. "Why is the recipe notebook in your briefcase anyway, Tom? It's supposed to stay in Mrs. Winkles's office when we're not using it." Meg reached down and pulled out the bright red notebook. Several pages fluttered to the floor.

Tom scrambled to pick them up, but Meg got to them first.

"What are all these copies doing here, Tom?" Meg asked. "You just finished telling me I shouldn't need to read the recipes anymore. Why do you need so many copies?"

Tom looked away from Meg only to find the Aldens staring at him. They were wondering the same thing.

"I . . . uh . . . well, I wanted to make sure the Aldens here had some copies . . ." Tom said, "in case they needed to make up some candy batches."

Meg put her hands on her hips. "I don't think Mrs. Winkles would have them do that without one of us here. You'd better give me those. Everything is supposed to stay in the factory when we're not using the recipes."

Tom tried to get hold of the papers, but Meg was too quick for him. "I guess the pages got mixed up with other stuff in my briefcase," he said in a quiet voice.

Benny noticed something odd on Tom's briefcase. "Hey, somebody made a mistake on the tag. It says *T.W.* I know my letters now. Shouldn't it be *T.C.* for *Tom Chipley?*"

Tom flipped over the leather tag with the gold initials Benny had been reading. "This belonged to my grandfather. Tom . . . um . . . White."

By this time, Meg had gathered up all the recipe copies. She stuffed them into Mrs.

Winkles's notebook and put it safely in the file cabinet. "Okay, everybody out. I'm locking up."

Meg waved Tom and the Aldens out the door. She pulled it firmly behind her.

Tom snapped his briefcase shut and locked it with a small key.

The Aldens weren't sure why. His briefcase was completely empty.

CHAPTER 10

2 Good 2 B True

The day after they returned from the food show, Grandfather and Mrs. Winkles joined the children for breakfast up in the loft.

"I have a surprise," Mrs. Winkles announced as soon as the children cleared the breakfast dishes. She spread out all kinds of candy on the table. "You children are in for a treat—in fact, you're in for a lot of them. I brought back wonderful, old-fashioned candies that other candy makers have been making in this area for a long time. Help yourselves, now that you've had a good breakfast."

"Some of these candies have been around since I was a boy," Grandfather told his grandchildren. "Peanut butter buckeyes, chocolate jelly sticks — those are a hundred years old."

"Is it still okay to eat them?" Soo Lee asked.

James Alden laughed. "Well, only the candy brands have been around for over a hundred years. The candies themselves are all freshly made."

As the children enjoyed their treats, they took turns helping Mrs. Winkles catch up on the news around the factory.

"What about the strange candy hearts that wound up in my shipment?" Mrs. Winkles asked.

Benny hated to set aside his chocolate jelly stick, but he was bursting with news. "We have lots of clues. Not just about hearts, either. You know those little candy ghosts that go in those chocolate pumpkins you send us on Halloween? Some of them got mixed in with the little candy chicks. But don't worry. We found all of them."

Mrs. Winkles put down her cup. She felt too upset to enjoy her morning coffee. "Oh, my. Thank goodness for that."

"We haven't quite figured out who mixed up the candies or messed up the mice," Jessie said. "We have a feeling Mr. Boxer has something to do with it — and that Meg or Tom might be working with him."

Jessie paused. She didn't really want to give Mrs. Winkles any more bad news. "We think Mr. Boxer might be making candy, also. The inspector went there and— "

"Mr. Boxer making candy?" Mrs. Winkles asked. "My goodness, perhaps that's why he never allows me past his office and always tells me to call ahead before I visit."

"If it's okay with you," Henry said, "we want to go over there with Meg and Tom but not tell them why."

Violet could see that hearing Tom's name upset Mrs. Winkles. "I don't think Tom's done anything wrong. He just gets upset sometimes."

Mrs. Winkles was grateful to Violet. "Oh, I do know what you mean. He's usually so friendly and helpful. Other times . . . well, if we get talking about personal matters, he just clams right up. I'll just tell him and Meg I need them to come on some errands with me — that I have some business to do and it can't wait."

When everyone arrived at Boxer's Shipping Company, the air was filled with the smell of chocolate.

The Aldens watched Meg and Tom closely. Did they know what was going on?

"Why did you bring us here?" Meg asked Mrs. Winkles. "I need to get back to the candy factory. I don't want to fall behind."

"We'll go back soon," Mrs. Winkles told Meg. "Right now, I'd like to find Mr. Boxer."

The Aldens hurried over to Mr. Boxer's candy-making building.

"I want to catch him making candy," Henry whispered.

Jessie crept up to the window of the

candy kitchen first. She stood on her tip-toes. "Mr. Boxer has the chocolate sprayers going. Look."

That was enough for Henry. He walked to the door, knocked on it, and pushed it open.

Mr. Boxer rushed over. "You kids again?" he shouted. "You can't come in here. I'm busy right now." When he started to push the door shut, Mr. Boxer spotted Mrs. Winkles. "Oh, excuse me, Mrs. Winkles. I didn't know you were coming."

Mr. Boxer didn't scare off Jessie. She stepped into the candy kitchen right after Henry. "You're making candy." She looked around at the dozens of metal egg molds slowly moving along a conveyor belt.

Benny picked up an egg carton that was already filled with chocolate eggs. "These are just like Mrs. Winkles's chocolate eggs, too."

"Well, they're not. They're Boxer's chocolate eggs," Mr. Boxer blurted out.

Meg pushed her way past the Aldens. She took a closer look at the chocolate egg carton Benny was holding. "I gave you the name of the place that makes those cartons."

"Meg!" Mrs. Winkles cried. "How could you do that?"

Meg leaned against the counter. Her face was pale. "Mr. Boxer said he sometimes needed extra cartons in case yours got dented or there were other problems with them. I didn't know he would put his own name on the cartons!"

Mr. Boxer exploded. "Problems, Meg? My only problem was hiring someone who never had a real job before, who kept giving my men the wrong directions, mixing up orders, taking down the wrong phone messages. There was no end to the problems. Getting you to spill information about Mrs. Winkles's factory was easy — like taking candy from a baby."

Meg swallowed hard. She went from being pale to red-faced. "You planted me at Winkles Candy Factory to spy for you?" she said, her voice rising. "That's why you were always asking me questions and bothering me about how Mrs. Winkles did things? So you could start your own business?"

Mr. Boxer put his hands up as if to push away Meg and her words. "Out of here, everyone. This is nobody's business but mine. And there's plenty of candy business for everyone. Selling candy to schools, for example. There's enough room for me and my candy."

"As long as you do it fair and square," Mrs. Winkles said. "Sending a young person out to spy for you isn't the way to do good business, Mr. Boxer."

For the first time, Mr. Boxer looked a little ashamed. But only a little.

"I don't care what you think of me," he said angrily. "And I don't care what a bunch of kids have to say." And with that, he turned away from them.

Realizing they weren't getting anywhere with Mr. Boxer, the Aldens turned their attention back to Meg. They weren't done with her, either. "You gave us the wrong key and wrong information about things — like you didn't want us to see what you were up to," Jessie said.

"And what about not wearing your gloves when the inspector came?" Henry added.

"And letting a cat in while he was there?" Benny pointed out. "Don't forget that."

Meg looked at the Aldens, then at Mrs. Winkles. "I didn't do any of those things on purpose. Sometimes, when I try too hard, I make mistakes," Meg confessed. "I was afraid to ask questions or ask for help, so I kept messing up. It got worse after all the Aldens showed up. They watched every single thing I did and asked a million questions."

Mrs. Winkles looked right at Meg. "That's how you learn, Meg — by watching, asking questions, and paying close attention. You didn't have to pretend you knew things you didn't know. That just made your job much harder."

Meg looked miserable. "I was worried you'd fire me and give Tom my job. He seemed to know everything."

"Why did you talk to Mr. Boxer on the phone so much?" Jessie asked.

Now it was Meg's turn to look angry. She turned to Mr. Boxer. "You kept calling me all the time as if you were still my boss. Sometimes I couldn't think straight — I even forgot to put my gloves on when the inspector came. You made it so hard for me to keep my mind on my work."

Mr. Boxer didn't look a bit sorry anymore, just impatient to get rid of everybody.

No one budged until Henry noticed someone was missing. "Where's Tom in all this?" he asked.

"Outside," Violet said. "He just left. Where are you going, Tom?" Violet called out the door.

Henry moved toward the door as well. "If Meg isn't the one who helped Mr. Boxer, then Tom must have something to do with all the problems."

"Not Tom," Violet and Mrs. Winkles said at the same time.

"That guy?" Mr. Boxer said. "He's just a snoop, always checking around here until I told him to stay away. Don't worry, he doesn't work for me. I could've used a smart guy like that, too. But he only wanted to work at Winkles — like it belonged to his family or something."

"The briefcase!" Jessie smacked her forehead. "The initials on Tom's briefcase said: *T.W.* Remember?"

"Let's get out of here and go find Tom," Henry said, glaring at Mr. Boxer. "We've done what we came here to do."

"You're right," said Mrs. Winkles. "I don't think Mr. Boxer will be causing any more trouble."

The Aldens caught up to Tom out in the parking lot.

Tom turned away from everyone. "Leave me be," he said. "Not that I blame you for looking at me like that — like I hurt Mrs. Winkles's business on purpose."

"Did you?" Violet asked. "Somebody put candy hearts with scary messages into Mrs. Winkles's shipments. And mixed in Halloween ghosts with the sugar chicks."

"And somebody squished the little chocolate mice," Soo Lee added.

Tom looked completely confused. "I wasn't that somebody."

Meg's eyes widened. "It must have been Mr. Boxer again! One time I found him with some open boxes from other candy factories. He said the deliveryman dropped some shipments and candy fell out. But he was the only one who could have mixed up the Halloween candies with the candy hearts and eggs."

"And he must have been the one who put the hearts with scary message into Mrs. Winkles's shipments," said Henry.

Violet smiled at Tom. "I knew it wasn't you."

Violet's words didn't seem to make Tom feel any better. "I didn't lie about the candy, but I wasn't completely honest about something else," Tom said miserably.

"You'd better explain what you mean by that," Henry said.

"I've often had the feeling you were holding something back, Tom," Mrs. Winkles said. "What was it?"

"And who's *T.W.* anyway?" Benny asked. "Jessie saw that on your briefcase, but you're a *T.C.* I know how to read."

The Aldens thought they saw Tom smile a little bit.

"I guess I never should have come to Mrs. Winkles's factory," Tom said when he saw everyone waiting for an answer. "I'd better come clean about who I am and who I'm not."

"You're not Tom Chipley?" Violet asked.

Jessie's jaw dropped, and before Tom could answer, she said: "The *W* on your briefcase stands for *Winkles*, doesn't it? I've been wondering and wondering about that ever since we saw you in Mrs. Winkles's office with her candy recipes."

"They're family recipes," Tom said. "*My* family's recipes as well as yours, Mrs. Winkles. I'm Tom Winkles, Junior."

Mrs. Winkles took a deep breath. "What do you mean?"

"My dad and my aunt are Seth Winkles's brother and sister. We all live in Lititz now," Tom began. "They went into the baking business after Uncle Seth left the candy factory to you and not them. I started to tell you that's what I did, but when you thought I said *banker*, not *baker*, it made it easier than telling you who I really was. I'm so sorry."

"Your father and aunt always told Seth they didn't want the business. That's why he left it to me." Mrs. Winkles looked more upset than the Aldens had ever seen her. "I even wrote to them saying I wouldn't mind sharing some of the old family recipes and such. But they never answered my letters."

Tom put his hand on Mrs. Winkles's arm. "The two of them are too darn stubborn and proud. But once the factory was gone, they decided they wanted it after all. Go figure."

"I told my daddy I didn't want my red wagon, but when he gave it away, I did want it," Soo Lee announced.

"Oh, yes," Mrs. Winkles said. "That's the way these things often go. What I don't understand, Tom, is why you didn't just tell me who you were — why you were so secretive. And why you turned up now, after so many years."

Henry answered before Tom. "I have a feeling I know. It's like when Grandfather tried to find us. We wanted to stick together with each other — to be our own family."

"That's exactly right," Tom agreed. "My dad and Aunt Millie are getting older now. They depend on me. They'd be upset if they knew I was here. I gave myself six months to learn all about candy making. I just thought I could find some of the old recipes and add some new items to our line of baked goods. I want to make a success of our business for them — expand it."

The Aldens believed Tom, but they still had a question.

"What about the broken part on the chick machine?" Jessie asked. "And not talking to us the morning we saw you?"

Tom looked down at his shoes. "I'm sorry about that, Jessie. Like Meg, I wanted to handle any problems myself. I guess I was hoping if Meg left, Mrs. Winkles would hire me to manage the factory, and I'd get around to telling her the truth."

"It gets harder to do that the longer the lie goes on, doesn't it?" James Alden said.

"It sure does," Tom answered. "I went back early in the morning to try to fix the machine, but I didn't have enough time. I was hoping to get away before anybody saw me. But you Aldens were too quick."

"And Mr. Boxer was too quick getting away from us," Jessie said. "I'd like to find him and get him to admit all the things he did."

"I don't want to see him again," Mrs. Winkles said. "It doesn't matter to me what Mr. Boxer says or does from now on. Now I know why Meg was so nervous around the factory. With Mr. Boxer out of the picture, I know she'll do a great job. The most important thing is I found my nephew, Tom."

"And I found you, Mrs. Winkles," Tom said.

"You mean Aunt Rose, don't you?" Mrs. Winkles asked. "You'd better start calling me that if you want to work in the family business — maybe even open a Winkles Candy Factory branch in Lititz."

"Okay, Mrs. — I mean, Aunt Rose," Tom said. "I know that with you, me, Meg, and the Aldens here, Mr. Boxer won't have a chance with that school contract."

The Aldens laughed and clapped.

Benny sniffed the sugary air. "Well, I'm glad that mystery is all figured out. I'm hungry."

Mrs. Winkles reached into her purse and pulled out a box of Winkles candy hearts. "Here, have some of these."

Benny flipped open the box top, took out a heart, and read what it said. Then he held up the candy box with one hand and made talking motions with his other hand.

"Do you want us to guess the message on the candy heart?" Violet asked.

Benny nodded.

"*Sugar*," Henry guessed.

"*Chatterbox*," Soo Lee said.

"*Talk to Me*," guessed Jessie.

"I've got it!" Violet said. "*Sweet Talk*."

Benny grinned. "Violet guessed right. My candy heart says, *Sweet Talk*. Now that we solved our candy mysteries, that's all we'll hear at Winkles Candy Factory."

The Sweet Smell of Success

The Aldens love candy — who doesn't? They look forward to their trip to the Winkles Candy Factory because it combines two favorite things: sweet treats and mysteries! They're not sure what's happening at the factory, but they're determined to get to the bottom of the mystery. They're not going to let anyone put Mrs. Winkles out of business!

Now you can test your own sleuthing skills in the puzzles provided. Grab your pencils and sink your (sweet) teeth in. You can check your answers at the back of the book. Good luck and sweet dreams!

Chocolate Mice

Mrs. Winkles knows that presentation is a very important part of the candy business. The candy has to look good enough to eat! These chocolate mice are ready to ship out. Before they get packed up, take a closer look. One of these is not like the others and shouldn't leave the factory. Can you circle the mouse that doesn't make the cut?

What Can You Make from Chocolate?

The Aldens helped Mrs. Winkles make different types of candy from chocolate. What else can you make from chocolate? Try rearranging the letters in the word to create new three-, four-, and five-letter words. If you can get to thirty, you're ready for the conveyor belt!

CHOCOLATE

_____   _____
_____   _____
_____   _____
_____   _____
_____   _____
_____   _____
_____   _____
_____   _____
_____   _____
_____   _____
_____   _____
_____   _____
_____

A-Mazing Fudge

The Aldens are making a big batch of fudge. They've put all the ingredients in the giant kitchen mixer and left it running while they check out the rest of the factory. Ooops! Suddenly, Violet realizes that they've left out the vanilla! Help the children get back to the kitchen to add the vanilla before it's too late!

Conveyor Belt Mix-up

Mrs. Winkles's candy factory has already had one mix-up too many. Help the Aldens straighten out the conveyor belt lines. Draw a line connecting the proper filling to the proper shell. Candy hearts belong in hollow hearts; candy chicks belong in hollow chicks; candy ghosts belong in hollow skeletons; and candy canes belong in hollow Christmas trees.

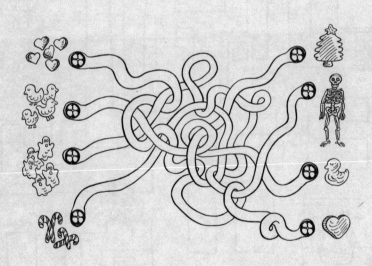

Sweet Talk

It's a rainy Saturday afternoon and the Aldens are inside playing. They're bored with checkers and chess, so Henry comes up with a new game. First, he dumps the candy hearts on the table. Then, he challenges his siblings to make as many sentences as possible with the words. Using the word list below, how many can you come up with?

I   DEAR   SEE   DOG   RUN   CATCH   YOU

MY   DESK   CANDY   LIKE   TO   FOR   SMALL

....

....

....

....

....

....

....

....

Sweet Search

The Aldens love a mystery, and they've cooked up a great one here. There are ten candy words hidden in the puzzle. Can you circle them all? The words go up and down and left to right.

candy   heart   chocolate   sweet   sugar
fudge   egg   bar   yummy   kitchen

C H O C O L A T E K S
A E R F Y D R Y G U Y
N A J U H K S U G A R
D R P D B A R M N S C
Y T H G D A L M Q H I
S W E E T P H Y F B E
W O K I T C H E N Z G

Another Mix-up!

Just when the Aldens thought they'd solved the mysterious happenings at the candy factory, here's another mix-up! The letters of these candy words are all scrambled. Can you unscramble them and write them correctly on the lines provided?

gudfe _____

hoclaeotc _____

tusn _____

lainval _____

gusra _____

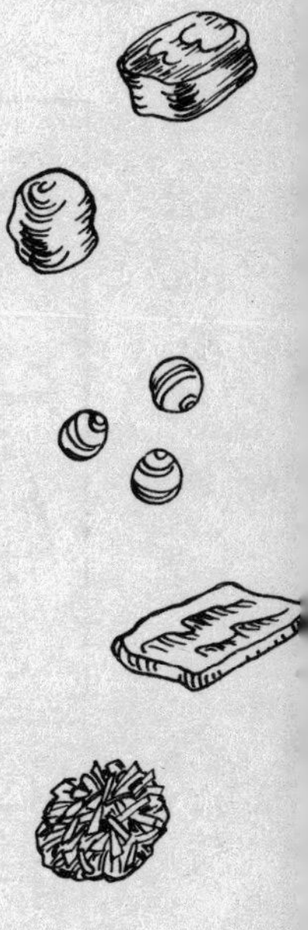

What's Hiding in the Egg?

In their apartment over the candy factory, the Aldens worry about Mrs. Winkles and her business. Someone is trying to cause her problems by hiding the wrong types of candy in hollow eggs. Can you find and circle the candies hidden in the picture? You'll find a chick, a ghost, a mouse, and a duck.

Heart to Heart

It all started with the conversation hearts. The Aldens discovered that someone was mixing up Mrs. Winkles's supplies. There are fifteen candy hearts hidden in the scene below. Can you find and circle all of them?

A Sweet Test

The Aldens learned a lot about making candy during their stay at Mrs. Winkles's factory. Did you? Test your memory by answering the questions below.

1. What does Mrs. Winkles require all her kitchen workers to wear?
    (a) sneakers   (b) shirts   (c) gloves

2. Liquid chocolate is poured into what to make different shapes?
    (a) molds   (b) bags   (c) milk cartons

3. During its creation, candy travels on these throughout the factory:
  (a) roller skates   (b) conveyor belts   (c) sleds

4. Violet notices candy left on a loading dock at Mr. Boxer's. What is she afraid will hurt the candy?
  (a) the sun   (b) loud noises   (c) trick-or-treaters

5. Benny eats too much of what kind of chocolate?
    (a) chocolate pens   (b) chocolate eggs
                (c) chocolate socks

Answer Key

Chocolate Mice

Mouse #4 cannot be shipped

What Can You Make from Chocolate?

Possible words include:

late	cola	eat	lot	act
cocoa	coal	teal	let	echo
talc	tale	cleat	chat	hole
coat	tea	cheat	cot	clot
ate	toe	heat	hate	hotel
oat	cat	hat	hoe	teach

A-Mazing Fudge

Conveyor Belt Mix-Up

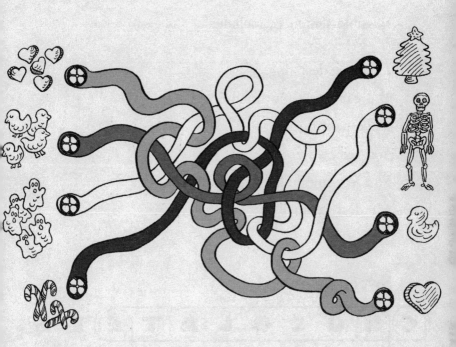

Sweet Talk

Possible sentences include:

I see my dear dog.

You can catch my small dog.

I like to run.

You see candy?

You like my desk?

My desk is small.

Sweet Search

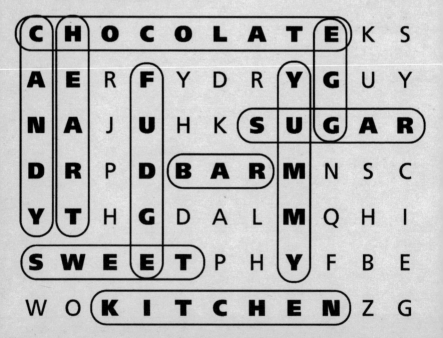

Another Mix-up!

<u>fudge</u>

<u>chocolate</u>

<u>nuts</u>

<u>vanilla</u>

<u>sugar</u>

What's Hiding in the Egg?

Heart to Heart

A Sweet Test

1. (c) gloves
2. (a) molds
3. (b) conveyor belts
4. (a) the sun
5. (b) chocolate eggs

GERTRUDE CHANDLER WARNER discovered when she was teaching that many readers who like an exciting story could find no books that were both easy and fun to read. She decided to try to meet this need, and her first book, *The Boxcar Children*, quickly proved she had succeeded.

Miss Warner drew on her own experiences to write the mystery. As a child she spent hours watching trains go by on the tracks opposite her family home. She often dreamed about what it would be like to set up housekeeping in a caboose or freight car — the situation the Alden children find themselves in.

When Miss Warner received requests for more adventures involving Henry, Jessie, Violet, and Benny Alden, she began additional stories. In each, she chose a special setting and introduced unusual or eccentric characters who liked the unpredictable.

While the mystery element is central to each of Miss Warner's books, she never thought of them as strictly juvenile mysteries. She liked to stress the Aldens' independence and resourcefulness and their solid New England devotion to using up and making do. The Aldens go about most of their adventures with as little adult supervision as possible — something else that delights young readers.

Miss Warner lived in Putnam, Connecticut, until her death in 1979. During her lifetime, she received hundreds of letters from girls and boys telling her how much they liked her books.